SCOOBY-DOO! A Haunted Halloween

Adapted by Lee Howard
Illustrations by Alcadia Snc
(Michela Burzo, Lisa Amerighi, Elena Prearo, Marzia Mariani)
Based on the episode "A Scooby-Doo Halloween" by Nahnatchka Khan

ISBN 978-0-545-36864-3

12 11 10 9 8 7 6 5 4 3 2 1   11 12 13 14 15/0

Designed by Henry Ng
Printed in the U.S.A.   40
First printing, July 2011

D0888232

SCHOLASTIC INC.

New York   Toronto   London   Auckland
Sydney   Mexico City   New Delhi   Hong Kong

It's the night before Halloween, and Scooby and the gang are on their way to visit Velma's aunt. Her town, Banning Junction, is celebrating its 100th anniversary.

ONLY 23 HOURS AND 59 MINUTES UNTIL HALLOWEEN NIGHT!

But when the gang arrives, they discover the townspeople aren't very happy to see them.

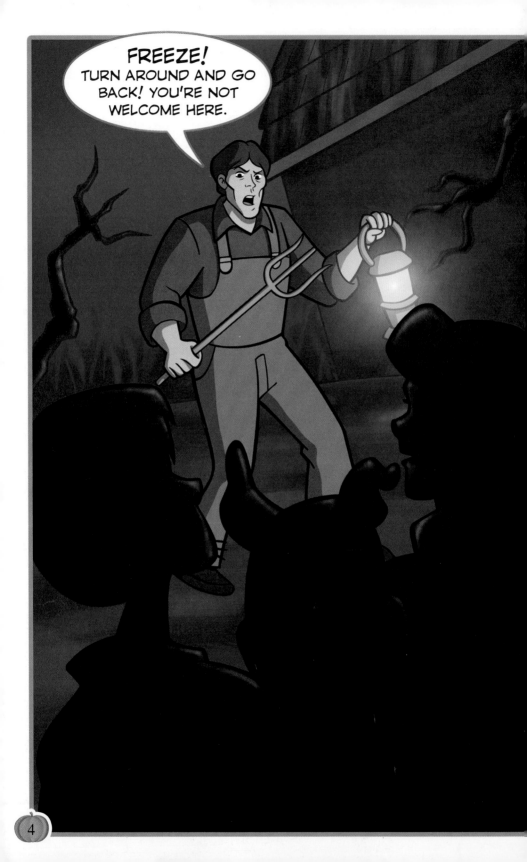

Velma's aunt Meg and uncle Evan recognize the kids just in time.

WAIT, IT'S VELMA! SORRY, WE DIDN'T MEAN TO SCARE YOU. IT'S JUST THAT SOMEONE'S BEEN BURNING OUR CORNFIELDS.

Aunt Meg and Uncle Evan bring the kids back to their house. Their daughter rushes out to greet them.

HI, COUSIN MARCY!
LONG TIME, NO SEE!
WHY IS EVERYONE
SO SCARED?

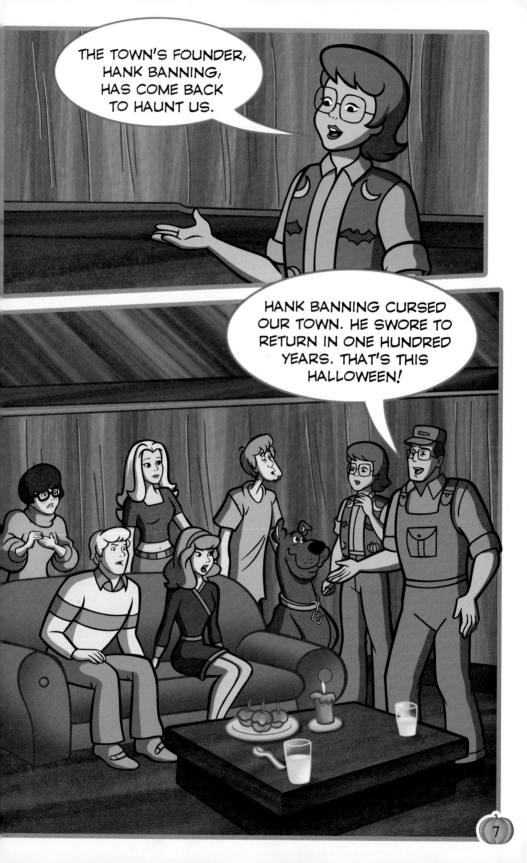

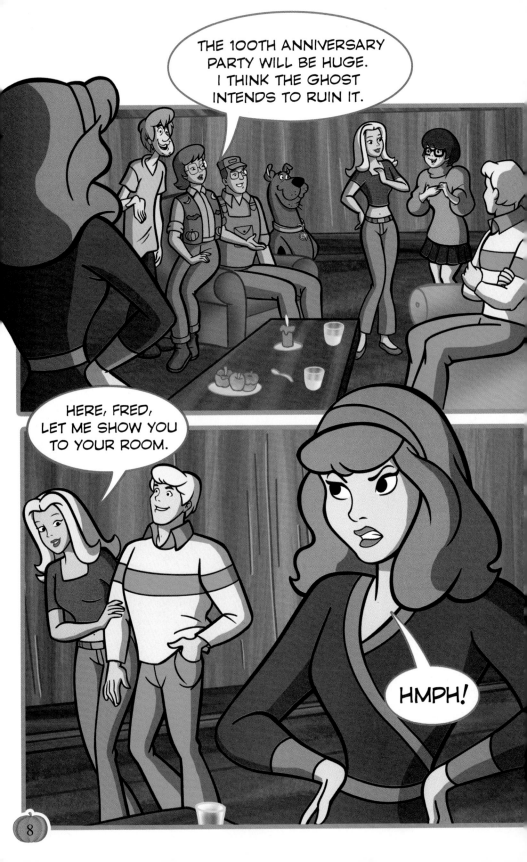

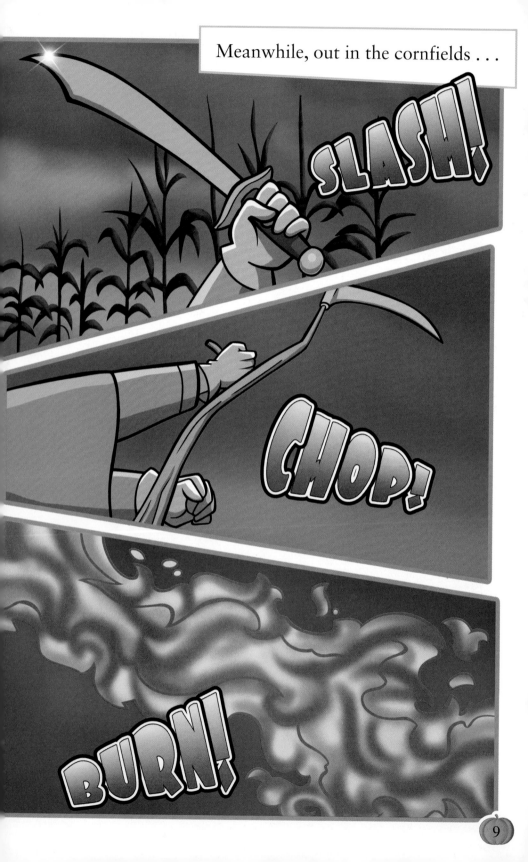

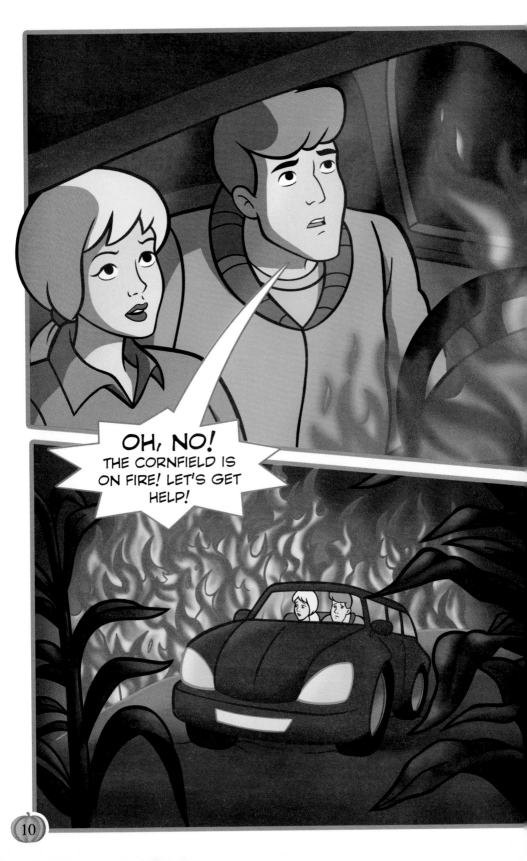

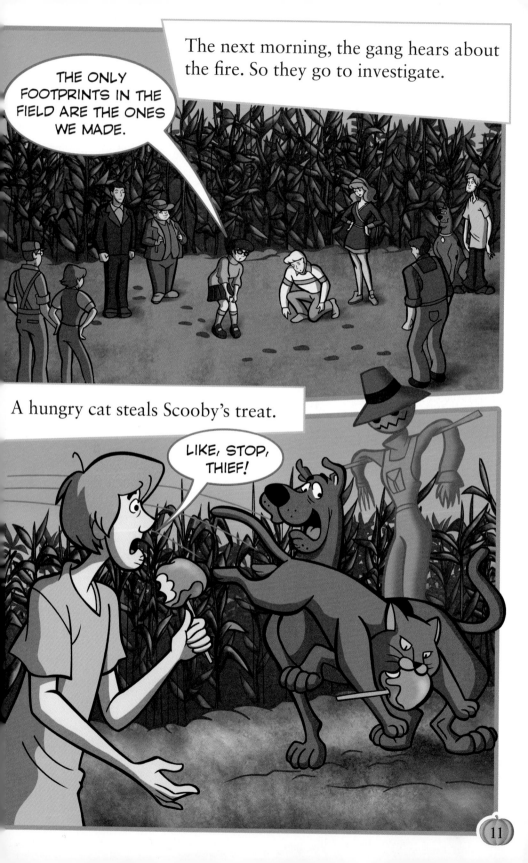

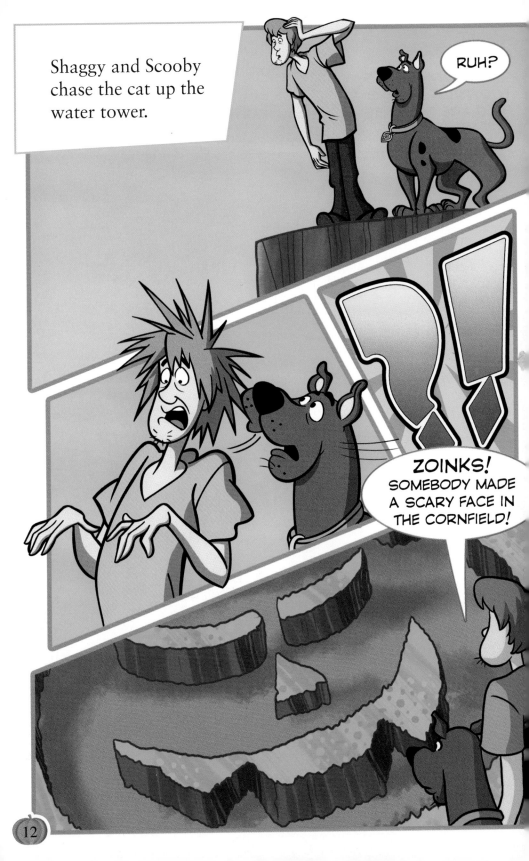

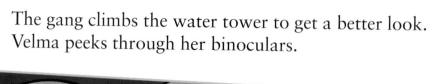

The gang climbs the water tower to get a better look. Velma peeks through her binoculars.

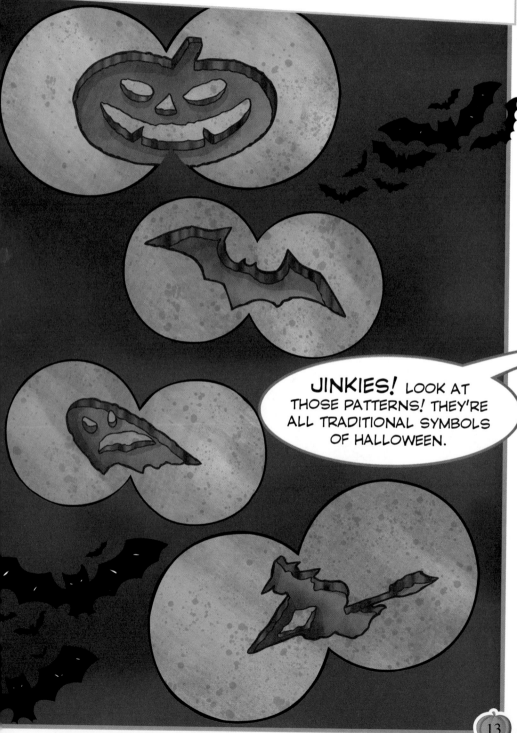

JINKIES! LOOK AT THOSE PATTERNS! THEY'RE ALL TRADITIONAL SYMBOLS OF HALLOWEEN.

When the gang climbs down from the water tower, a creepy-looking woman is waiting for them.

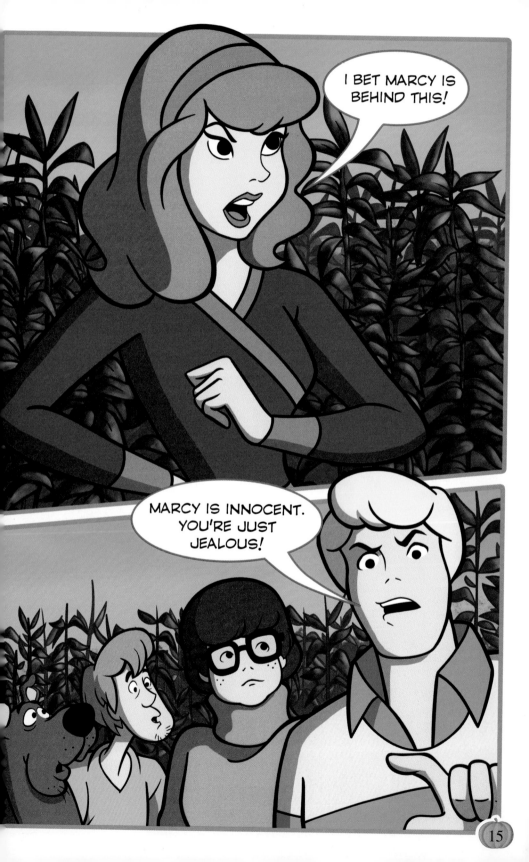

The gang splits up to look for clues. Shaggy and Scooby head to the old woman's house.

LIKE, I BET THAT CREEPY OLD LADY IS BEHIND ALL THIS.

DIDN'T YOUR MAMAS EVER TEACH YOU TO KNOCK?

Meanwhile, Fred, Daphne, and Velma investigate at the library.

HANK BANNING WAS MAYOR FOR THIRTY YEARS. THEN HE WAS VOTED OUT OF OFFICE. HE DIED ON HALLOWEEN NIGHT, SWEARING TO RETURN AND SEEK HIS REVENGE!

As they leave the library, the gang bumps into Marcy. She's studying for her electrical engineering class.

WHERE WERE YOU THIS MORNING?

TODAY IS MY BIRTHDAY, BUT I WAS WORKING AT THE MALL. I'M ON THE SECURITY TAPE. SEE FOR YOURSELF.

Fred and the girls head to the mall. The security tape clearly shows Marcy working.

That night, the gang explores the cornfield.
COME ON GUYS, LET'S FIND SOME CLUES.
JEEPERS! LOOK AT THAT SCARECROW! IT'S ALIVE!

Suddenly, all the scarecrows come alive!

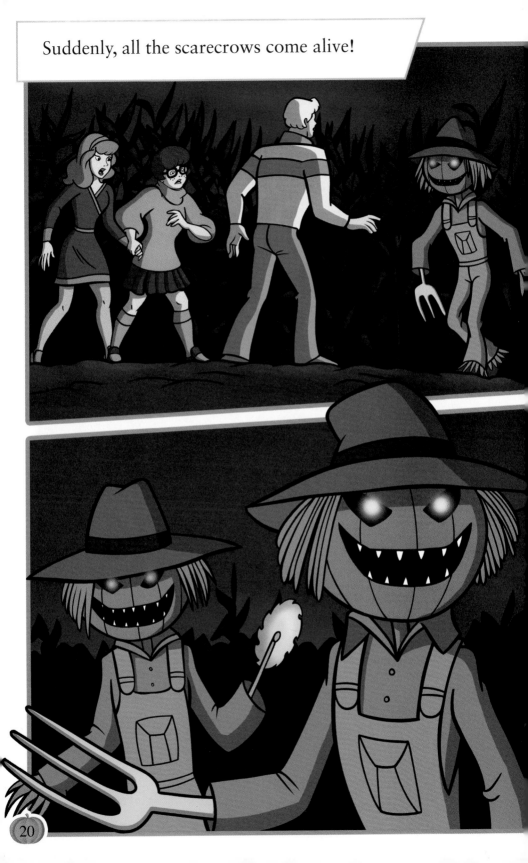

The gang heads for the old barn, but the doors are locked.

LIKE, RUN FOR YOUR LIVES!

YIKES!

WE'RE CORNERED!

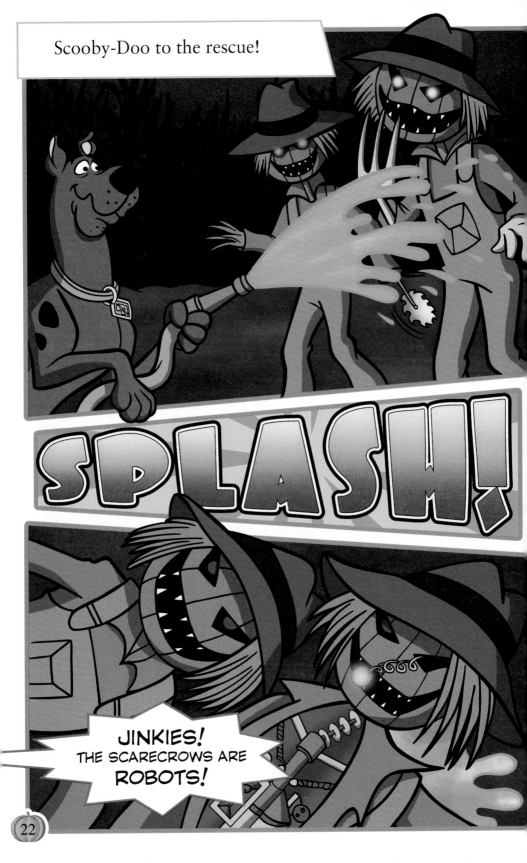

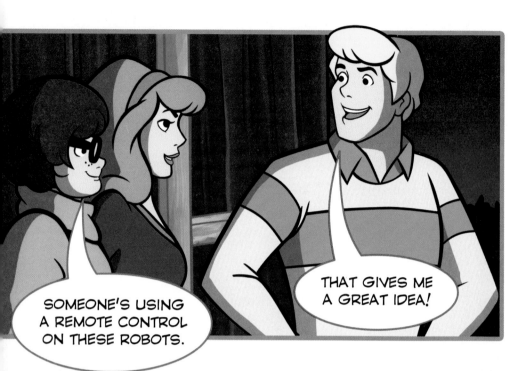

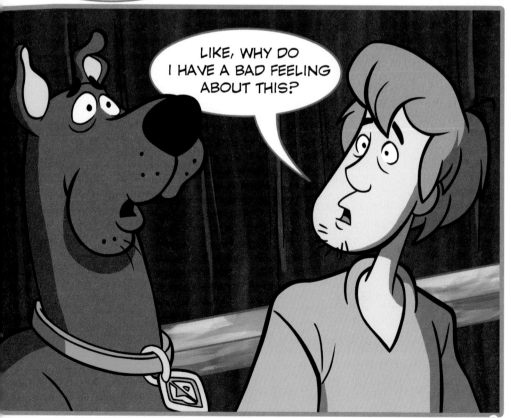

The next thing they know, Shaggy and Scooby are disguised as robots. They try to blend in.

Meanwhile, in the Mystery Machine, Velma monitors the remote control transmission.

I'VE GOT IT! THE SIGNAL IS COMING FROM INSIDE TOWN HALL.

Over at Town Hall, the anniversary party is in full swing. Until . . . a ghost appears!

Fred, Velma and Daphne throw pumpkins at the ghost, but the pumpkins fly right through him!

The scarecrow robots start to attack the guests! Shaggy and Scooby chase them away with apples.

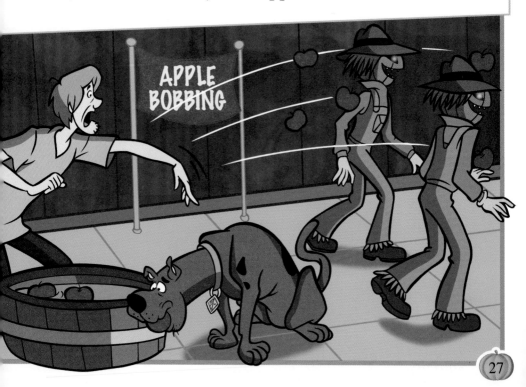

APPLE BOBBING

Two scarecrows close in on Shaggy!

SCOOBY-DOO! WHERE ARE YOU?!

Scooby swings to the rescue and saves his best buddy.

THE GHOST IS A PROJECTION!

The gang checks out the projection room — but nobody's there!

WHO WOULD GO TO ALL THIS TROUBLE TO UPSTAGE HALLOWEEN?

Velma has an idea.

The gang heads to the water tower and catches Marcy red-handed!

REMEMBER THE GLOVE FROM THE WATER TOWER? I SAW ONE JUST LIKE IT ON THE SECURITY TAPE. MARCY LEARNED HOW TO BUILD THE SCARECROWS IN HER ELECTRICAL ENGINEERING CLASS. THEN SHE PROGRAMMED THEM TO BURN HALLOWEEN PATTERNS IN THE CORNFIELDS.

THANKS TO VELMA, WE STILL HAVE TIME TO GO TRICK-OR-TREATING!

After a night of Halloween mystery, the gang jumps into the Mystery Machine. As they drive away, they pass Marcy on the side of the road.